LIBRARY AND ARCHIVES CANADA CATALOGUING IN PUBLICATION

Jovanovic, Katarina, 1962-, author
  The blue vase / Katarina Jovanovic ; illustrated by Josée Bisaillon.
ISBN 978-1-896580-91-3 (pbk.)

  I. Bisaillon, Josée, 1982-, illustrator II. Title.

PS8619.O86B58 2015   jC813'.6   C2015-902988-0

Book design by Elisa Gutiérrez
This book was typeset in Urge Text
and Pacific Northwest Letters

10 9 8 7 6 5 4 3 2 1
Printed and bound in Canada.

MIX
Paper from
responsible sources
FSC® C016245
www.fsc.org

The publisher thanks the Government of Canada and Canadian Heritage for their financial support through the Canada Council for the Arts, the Canada Book Fund and Livres Canada Books. The publisher also thanks the Government of the Province of British Columbia for the financial support it has given through the Book Publishing Tax Credit program and the British Columbia Arts Council.

Canada Council
for the Arts

Conseil des Arts
du Canada

BRITISH
COLUMBIA
ARTS COUNCIL

Katarina Jovanovic

THE BLUE VASE

illustrations by Josée Bisaillon

TRADEWIND BOOKS

Vancouver · London

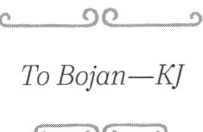

To Bojan—KJ

Contents

CHAPTER 1

An Accident

"Here, Sonia, take a couple of cookies," said Mrs. Kaminski, putting a plate with three warm sugary cookies in front of me.

"Thanks."

Before and after school, while my parents worked, I stayed with Mrs. Kaminski, our next-door neighbour. That afternoon, I was drinking tea in her kitchen. She was cooking nonstop, as usual. This was her way of earning a living; she worked for a catering company, making cabbage rolls, apple strudels and Polish dumplings called *perogies*. Mrs. Kaminski's short fat fingers were always covered in flour and salt, marmalade, icing sugar and oil. Her cheeks, flushed from the oven's heat, now were speckled with sugar crystals. Her eyes flitted back and forth to a small, black-and-white TV screen on the counter, where an old movie was playing loudly. One of her many cats, a black-and-white kitten, was staring at the TV screen with wide green eyes.

When I finished my snack, I walked into the living room. It contained all sorts of interesting things: old photos, figurines, antique clocks, music boxes and porcelain vases. Being in Mrs. Kaminski's living room felt like being in a museum. I especially loved looking at one of the paintings. It reminded me of the yellow wheat fields in the countryside outside Kisinau, in Moldova. Our family had moved from there to Vancouver two years ago.

Mrs. Kaminski's apartment was a lot like my grandmother's, with large rooms full of sunlight. Our dark and stuffy place here was so small that we had to keep most of our clothing, books and other belongings in big plastic containers. The only furniture was three beds, a floor lamp, and a small garden table with four chairs. Everything we owned could fit into the trunk of a large taxi.

I noticed something new in one of the cabinets: a beautiful blue-and-white vase. Painted onto it was a dramatic scene of a dark-blue sailing ship fighting a storm. The wild waves contrasted sharply with the vase's graceful curves. Suddenly, I felt like crying. The vase reminded me of the elegant things that my grandmother collected. I thought of the tea parties she used to invite me to—of her corn-flour cookies, and blueberries with whipped cream. Overcome with homesickness, I opened the cabinet's glass door and took out the magnificent vase.

I lifted it carefully with both hands. Normally, I didn't touch any of Mrs. Kaminski's precious things—but this time, I didn't care. I turned the vase around slowly. The deep ocean blue seemed to smell of lavender—just like my grandmother's house in the late summer. I closed my eyes and pressed my cheek against the cold porcelain.

All at once, someone opened the living room door. Startled, I dropped the vase. It shattered into hundreds of tiny pieces.

Marta, Mrs. Kaminski's granddaughter, was at my side in a moment, glaring at me. Her freckles stood out against the sudden redness of her face.

But it was weird; she seemed almost secretly pleased at the same time as she was angry.

She bent down and picked up a few of the fragments. "Look what you did! My grandma's gonna be furious!" she exclaimed, holding out the porcelain shards.

CHAPTER 2

Secret Pact

"How could you do that, Lasagne?" Marta shrieked.

She called me "Lasagne" to taunt me.

"You're in *really* big trouble now. Grandma's new vase came all the way from China. It was only delivered yesterday! She paid a lot of money for it. It was probably the only one like it in the whole world—and now you broke it!"

"I'm so sorry," I stammered. "I was just admiring it, and I didn't expect you to walk in." I was upset with myself for being so clumsy.

"Well, you had no business touching that vase in the first place!" Marta snapped. "Obviously you knew that, or you wouldn't have jumped when I came in. Now we have to break the news to my grandma, and I can tell you she's not going to like it. Not a bit! And your parents will have to pay for

a new one. It'll cost them a *fortune*. Grandma saved for *years* to buy that vase."

My heart started beating so hard that I was surprised Marta couldn't hear it. It was beating so fast that I thought it would leap right out of my chest. I was afraid I might die. I wished I could just vanish from the world—or wake up and realize that this was only a bad dream.

It wasn't.

But I didn't die and I didn't vanish. I had to face reality.

I apologized over and over again, but it didn't make any difference. Marta seemed to be enjoying the power she suddenly had over me.

"What can I *do*?" I asked her helplessly.

A little smile curled the corners of Marta's mouth. "Probably nothing. We'll just tell my grandma, and she'll speak to your parents. Maybe in a few years they'll be able to finish paying her back for your carelessness."

"But my parents will *never* have the money to pay for it! Can't we just glue this one back together?" I pleaded.

"Are you *nuts*? No way. It would show. Plus, we don't even have the right kind of glue."

I couldn't help it—I burst into tears.

"Unless—" whispered Marta.

That single word filled me with hope.

"Unless—we hide the pieces from my grandma."

"But won't she notice the vase is missing? You said she just got it yesterday." I was disappointed. I expected a more sensible solution.

"She probably won't notice it right away. She's going to be really busy in the kitchen for the next few days. Anyway, she's usually too tired to look around. And if she does, I'll just make up a story."

That will give me some time to figure out what to do.

"Thanks." I breathed. "You're a really good friend."

"Yeah, but you have to give me something in return for the favour."

"Like what?" I wondered anxiously. "I don't have any money."

"It doesn't have to be money." Marta seemed to be studying me for a minute. "For example, you could give me your erasers."

Not my eraser collection! Every time my mom got an extra tip at work, she bought me a new eraser to add to my collection. I already had twenty, of all different shapes and colours. I kept them in a pretty wooden case. I couldn't possibly give away gifts from my mom.

"I'm sorry, but there's no way I can give you my erasers. They mean too much to me. Except for one, I don't even use them to erase stuff; I just collect them. Maybe something else?"

"Then I guess I'll have to tell my grandma that you broke her precious antique vase."

The thought of my parents having to pay for such an expensive vase terrified me. Marta was my only hope.

"Okay, okay! Only, *please* don't tell your grandma! I'll bring my erasers tomorrow, I promise—if we can hide all these pieces before she comes in."

We gathered up all the blue porcelain fragments, and Marta stored them in a plastic bag that she hid at the back of her bedroom closet.

"Grandma won't look there," she explained.

When I got home, I carefully packed up my entire eraser collection and put it in my school bag.

My parents might have noticed that I was quiet at dinner, but they didn't say anything.

I did my homework and then read a bit of my favourite book. I tried not to think any more about the vase.

CHAPTER 3

Sticks And Stones

When I arrived at Mrs. Kaminski's the next morning, the place looked like the scene of a crime. One of the cats had been sick all over the living room, and the sofa cushions were scattered everywhere. Mrs. Kaminski was scurrying between the living room and the bathroom, busily cleaning up the mess. Marta was putting the cat in a pet carrier, to take it to the veterinarian.

Mrs. Kaminski sent me to the kitchen to fetch some wet towels. As always, the TV was on, and the black-and-white kitten was watching a man and a woman hugging each other at a train station. A container of uncooked perogies, labelled WEST END KAYAKING CLUB LUNCH, sat on the counter.

The phone rang. No one answered it.

I returned to the living room with the wet cloths, and saw that there was no breakfast on the table.

As soon as Mrs. Kaminski turned her back, Marta hissed, "You better have brought my erasers!" I handed over my box of erasers without a word. I was too upset to speak. Marta hardly looked at it. She dumped it into her school bag without even thanking me. *At least that's the end of it.*

During recess I saw Marta in the hallway, whispering to Kelly and Larissa. The three of them formed a clique, part of the "in" crowd, and they were always gossiping. When I approached, they stopped talking, glared at me, and turned their backs. *They're gossiping about me.*

I pretended to ignore it. "Hi. Do you want to play outside?" I offered, a little too brightly.

There was no answer.

Then Larissa spat out, "I won't be friends with a thief."

"Who's a thief?" I asked in surprise.

"Who's a thief?" Kelly repeated mockingly.

"*You* are! Marta said you stole her grandmother's vase," sneered Larissa.

"What? That's—that's not true!" I spluttered. I meant to yell it, but my voice came out strangled. I felt my face burn. The hallway spun. *I must be dreaming this. It's a nightmare.* "It's a lie. I didn't steal anything!"

I stared at Marta as sternly as I could. *Why were Kelly and Larissa so willing to believe her lies?* I brushed away a tear that had started to fall.

"Can I talk to you for a sec?" I asked Marta.

"Go ahead, talk to me." Marta exchanged glances with Larissa and Kelly.

They giggled.

"Um, let's go outside," I said. "I want to talk to you *alone*, outside."

Marta rolled her eyes, but followed me into the playground anyway.

"What?" she barked, looking annoyed.

"Why are you doing this to me? I said I'm sorry and I paid you back. Wasn't my eraser collection enough? You know you're not telling them the truth."

"So?"

"*So?*" I echoed, in disbelief. "It hurts that you're spreading lies about me."

"So what? I can do whatever I like." Marta looked me straight in the eye.

"But—I gave you my erasers!"

"Big deal! You think that makes up for what you did?"

She walked away, leaving me standing in the empty schoolyard.

CHAPTER 4

Stolen Breakfast

The next day, Mrs. Kaminski's living room was back in order. The sun shone onto the glass cases, making the porcelain shapes inside them gleam. A pink-and-blue vase sat in the blue vase's place. I sighed in relief. *I hope Mrs. Kaminski won't notice the switch.*

Marta's grandma was in the kitchen, preparing an apple strudel. Through the door, I could see the kitten staring at the flickering onscreen images of two men fighting.

Marta sat at the dining room table, eating breakfast. She smiled as if there were nothing but friendship between us. "Pancakes!" she announced, her mouth full.

The pancakes looked scrumptious: golden, fluffy and perfectly round, like sunbeams.

In between bites, Marta demanded, "So? What did you bring me?"

I was stunned. "Nothing. Was I supposed to bring something?"

Marta stared at me as if I'd fallen from the moon.

"You didn't know you were *supposed to*? Am I *supposed* to protect you for nothing? What else can you give me, to pay for my silence?"

"What do you mean? I gave you my eraser collection. Wasn't that enough?"

"No, it *wasn't* enough. I already told you that. Today, I'll just take your breakfast. Tomorrow, bring me a dollar. And you'd better not tell anyone about the money, especially not your parents."

A dollar! Where will I get that?

Marta grabbed the plate that had been set out for me. The pancakes glistened with strawberry jam. She swiftly cut them into large chunks and forked them into her mouth. Then she placed the empty plate in front of me.

Next, she reached over and drank my milk, wiped her mouth with the back of her hand, and grinned.

CHAPTER 5

Life Without Erasers

The book report I was working on had more spelling mistakes than ever. Dad looked over my shoulder and sighed. "You will have to practise your writing. Please fix the mistakes—and this time, pay attention to your work."

After he left the room, I couldn't concentrate on my homework. All I could think about was the broken vase, and about Marta's lying to Kelly and Larissa. *Giving up my erasers was supposed to make everything all right. Now I've lost them for nothing! And how can I possibly get a dollar?*

My father's words made me feel terrible. I looked everywhere for an eraser. *Maybe I can find some loose change around too.* I searched the kitchen drawers and even my dad's toolbox. There were no erasers to be found—and no money either.

I decided to try the drawer in the kitchen table.

"What are you looking for?" asked Mom.

"An eraser," I mumbled.

"An eraser! I bought you at least twenty, all different shapes and colours. Where are they?"

"I lost them."

"All of them?"

"Yes. The whole box," I whispered, embarrassed. *In a way, it's true.*

"Just like that? I am surprised you do not look after the things you care about. What a waste. I am disappointed in you, Sonia."

I examined my mother's face. She wasn't just angry. She seemed puzzled, and sad too. My heart sank.

"You need to learn the value of things," remarked Dad, walking in.

I wish I could tell them what really happened.

"Now go finish your homework, and go right to bed."

As soon as I had rewritten my assignment, I stretched out on the sofa. Then I remembered something I once saw in a movie. I threw off the cushions and searched the sofa corners for loose change.

Three quarters, a dime and two nickels! A nickel short. I hope it's enough for Marta.

CHAPTER 6

School Blues

"So, do you have my money?" Marta demanded as we walked to school the next day.

I handed over the coins.

She counted them and scowled. "That's only ninety-five cents."

"That's all I could get."

"Next time, bring me exactly what I ask for."

For the next two weeks, Marta made me give her my recess snacks and even some of my lunches. And sometimes I'd find glue on my chair or a rotten banana in my lunchbox. Kelly and Larissa kept calling me "stupid" and said that I smelled like cabbage. Since they and Marta taunted and sometimes attacked me during recess and lunchtime, I started hiding. My usual places were the gym

equipment room, under the back stairway, or locked inside one of the washroom stalls.

One day in gym class, we were playing Red Rover. Marta's friend Larissa was on the other team. She ran straight between me and Emma, broke through the line, and crashed into the back wall, hurting her shoulder. The gym teacher sent Larissa to the school nurse.

Back in class, Kelly told a group of girls that I had pulled my hand away on purpose.

At lunchtime, no one sat with me. And I had nobody to play with outside after lunch either. As soon as I approached any kids, they scattered.

One day, I found a mushy egg-salad sandwich that someone had stuffed into my jacket pocket. It made a smelly disgusting mess.

After school, I tried to wash out the stain in Mrs. Kaminski's bathroom sink. But I couldn't get rid of it.

When I returned from the bathroom, Marta was rummaging through my school bag. "That's a nice set of pencil crayons you've got. I could really use them for my art project."

How would I ever explain this to my mother?
"No, you can't have them. My mom will be furious."

"Your mom will be even *angrier* if she has to pay for that vase!"

That night, my mother noticed the stain on my jacket and asked me what happened.

"Um, I forgot and left my sandwich in my pocket. I'm sorry."

"But there are bits of egg salad in the corners of the pocket. I gave you a *turkey* sandwich today, with mustard."

"I traded it with Emma. She didn't like her lunch."

My mom sighed. "Sonia, I don't want you to trade your sandwiches for someone else's."

"Sorry. I won't do it again."

"Good. But your jacket is ruined. The greasy stain shows on the outside too."

"Sorry," I mumbled.

I hate taking the blame for things that aren't my fault.

I ran to my room.

I didn't want to have to deal with Marta. I didn't want to hand over any more of my stuff. And I hated lying to my parents. *I'm not going back to that stupid school ever again!*

CHAPTER 7

Hoping For A Tornado

Every morning, I woke up dreading another day at school. At night, my chest was so tight that I almost expected it to burst.

Sometimes Mom believed my complaints of stomach ache, and let me stay at home. But usually, I dragged myself to school, hoping for a last-minute rescue—like a tornado, or even an earthquake. If everything came crashing down, that would be the beginning of my freedom. Then no one could blame me for a smashed vase. And if I didn't have to go to school, I wouldn't have to see Marta ever again.

Then I would be free.

Instead, every morning was perfectly ordinary.

Every lunchtime and recess, I went to one of my hiding spots, where I could stay unnoticed and safe.

The worst part of the day came after school, when I was alone with Marta. Every day, when her grandma served us a snack, Marta made me give her mine. It was difficult to watch her gobble it up when I was hungry.

Once in a while, Marta would lean close and whisper, "Grandma's friend came over yesterday and Grandma meant to show her the vase, but then luckily she got distracted and forgot"—or, "My grandma stared *right* at the spot where the vase used to be, but so far she hasn't said anything." That was the code for, "You need to bring me another small gift from home." Then I would have to give her a cuddly toy or some money. If I protested, Marta would stand up and head toward the kitchen, declaring that she couldn't keep my secret any longer.

At home, I invented stories about birthdays and school fairs, and stashed small items in my pockets and backpack. My mom sometimes looked at me strangely. I wondered if she was beginning to doubt my stories.

Sometimes I had nightmares in which I was ordered to stand and face the entire school during assembly. The principal would announce that carelessness, lying and breaking what didn't belong to you were proof of bad character. My cheeks would burn as all the teachers and children stared at me. Some of them whispered to each other and smirked. The whole school knew what I had done.

Other times, I dreamed that the blue vase from China still stood on its velvet stand, unbroken, its beautiful glaze glinting in the sun. In that dream, I was sitting alone in Mrs. Kaminski's living room, eating a snack of big strawberries dusted with brown sugar, with no worries at all.

CHAPTER 8

Lost And Found

Mrs. Dawson, the music teacher, looked at each of us in turn, like a hunter ready to pounce.

"I left the recorder right here on the desk," she announced, drumming her fingers on the spot three times. "When I came back after recess, it was gone. Does anyone know anything about this?"

She scanned our faces again, and waited.

"No one? *Someone* must know something, unless there's a ghost in the classroom."

Silence.

"Everyone will stay after school today, unless the recorder turns up before then."

Mrs. Dawson turned her attention to the tune we had begun learning the week before.

Kelly raised her hand. "Sonia took the recorder. I saw her. Just look in her knapsack!"

"I didn't steal anything!" I yelled. "Go ahead, check, if you don't believe me!" I took my knapsack from under my chair and handed it to Mrs. Dawson.

As she emptied its contents onto her desk, out tumbled the recorder.

I froze, astonished. Then I sputtered, "It wasn't me! I didn't take it. Someone must have put it there so I'd get blamed."

"Yeah, right!" a couple of kids snorted.

Mrs. Dawson eyed me sharply and said, "I'm afraid I'll have to meet with your parents. Now, class, let's continue where we left off."

That evening, I could smell the cherry blossoms in the front yard. I heard birdsong through the open window. Dad was laughing with a friend on the phone. Mom hugged me before taking my backpack to be washed. All at once, I felt lighter. Just like that, for no reason.

Then the phone rang. My mom answered it, and came back scowling a few minutes later.

"Sonia, what is this all about? That was your music teacher on the phone. She said you stole a recorder."

Should I tell her that school is torture? Or should I lie?

I felt very, very lonely. I knew that each new lie only pushed me deeper into that loneliness.

I looked straight at my mom. "Someone stole a recorder from the music room during recess and put it in my backpack."

Her dark eyes widened. "I don't understand. Why would anyone do such a thing?"

"To get me in trouble. A lot of the girls hate me."

"What do you mean, 'hate' you?"

"They say I'm stupid and that I smell like cabbage. One girl takes my lunches. I have to hide during lunchtime." I burst into sobs.

Mom took my face in her hands. "Look at me, Sonia."

I forced myself to meet her gaze. "They're mean to me and play tricks on me. Please tell the music teacher I didn't take the recorder."

. . .

My mom served an early dinner of cornbread, tomato soup and chicken. There wasn't much conversation at the table, but she and Dad kept exchanging glances. Afterward, I heard them talking in the kitchen while I did my homework. Dad came in later to give me an oatmeal cookie.

I slept next to my mother that night. Her arms were warm, and she smelled of lavender.

CHAPTER 9

Mrs. Dawson

The next morning, I woke up to the smell of freshly baked bread.

Mom was still wearing her nightgown, which meant she probably wasn't going to work that day. I was too pleased to ask her the reason.

"You are not going to Mrs. Kaminski's this morning," she announced. "We will go to school together, so I can talk to your music teacher about the recorder."

My excitement at the idea of staying home with Mom turned to dread. *What can Mom possibly tell Mrs. Dawson? We don't even know who put the recorder in my bag. The whole thing is hopeless.*

We walked to school in silence, hand in hand. My thoughts tumbled wildly and my lips were dry.

. . .

Mrs. Dawson was in the music room. She pulled up three chairs and, with an uncertain smile, sat down facing us. Her eyes looked cold.

I shuddered.

My mom looked uncomfortable on the small chair. She seemed to be preparing what she would say.

Mrs. Dawson shifted her attention to me. "Is there something you'd like to tell me, Sonia?" Her voice was sharp.

"Mrs. Dawson, I *didn't* take the recorder from your desk."

"Interesting. Then how do you think it got into your backpack?"

I shrugged. "I don't know. Someone put it there."

My mother interrupted. "I believe my daughter when she says she did not take it. I know my child, and I trust her. She would never steal."

"What makes you so confident? Children sometimes surprise us. They may be capable of things that seem out of character."

"Sonia told me last night that there are some girls at school who bother her. Maybe *they* put it in her bag."

Mrs. Dawson turned to me. "Sonia, I would like you to tell me everything you told your mother last night."

My tongue suddenly felt so huge that I was afraid I might choke. I was trembling. For no reason, I thought of Marta's guppies that had died, a little at a time, in their big clear jar.

I had no idea what to say. I shook my head.

"Okay, then just tell us this: who do you think might have taken the recorder and put it in your backpack?"

I shrugged again. I didn't actually know whether it was Marta, Kelly or Larissa who had done it. *Naming any of them will only land me in worse trouble, and Marta is sure to get back at me by telling her grandmother about the vase.*

My mother jumped in. "Sonia told me that some girls make fun of her and call her names. Maybe those girls played a trick on her."

Mrs. Dawson frowned, examined my face, and then rose from her chair. "Sonia, I believe that you didn't take the recorder."

"So can you watch now, to see that children do not bother my daughter anymore?" pleaded my mother.

"Mrs. Antonescu, perhaps you don't realize how many students we have here. It's not possible to supervise everyone at all times. It is the students' responsibility to tell us about any problems they are having." Mrs. Dawson turned to me. "When something like this happens, Sonia, you need to come to me or to another teacher, to tell us about it. Otherwise, we have no way of knowing. Okay?"

"Okay."

The teacher addressed my mom once again. "It is important that Sonia learns to stand up for herself. I wonder why she did not report any of these problems earlier. Could something else be upsetting her? Is everything all right at home?"

My mother bristled. "There is no trouble at home. We love each other very much and we are starting to feel settled here. We have been here for two years now."

Mrs. Dawson glanced at the wall clock. "I'm sorry, but my next class is about to begin. Sonia, if you have any more trouble with your friends, you can always come and talk to me."

I nodded. *They're not my friends.*

My mother kissed me and mumbled, "We'll talk later."

I went to my classroom feeling relieved. *At least Mrs. Dawson doesn't think I'm a thief.*

CHAPTER 10

Thoughts In A Furnace Room

Every day for three months, Marta ate my breakfasts and my snacks. She was taking *everything* from me: my personal stuff, my new school supplies and even the small gifts that my parents gave me once in a while. Sometimes she asked for my lunch too, if she liked it better than hers.

One morning Mrs. Kaminski brought us blueberry muffins, still warm from the oven. Marta grabbed my muffin, leaned in close and hissed, "If you ever tell anybody our secret, you'll be sorry. I mean it!"

She pinched me, then glanced at my school bag. "What do you have for lunch?"

"Tuna sandwich," I lied. Marta couldn't stand tuna sandwiches.

"Again?" she whined. "Tell your mom to make you something else for lunch. Tell her to make you

a turkey sandwich instead. I like it with mustard and pickles. For tomorrow."

"No. I won't." I was sick of her demands.

"I said: ask her! Or do you want me to *tell*? My grandma asked about the vase yesterday. She'll find out sooner or later, you know. I can't cover for you forever. I like turkey sandwiches, and you have to bring me what I want. I won't keep your lousy secret if you keep on bringing those disgusting tuna sandwiches!"

At lunchtime, I hid in the school's furnace room and ate the turkey sandwich that I had saved from Marta. Then I sat for a while in the dimly lit basement. The place smelled of oil and chemicals. It was warm but stuffy, and the floor was dirty. I tried not to think about how lonely I was. I stopped myself from crying. I didn't want to show up in class with my eyes red and swollen.

How much longer can this go on? There's no way to make things right.

CHAPTER 11

True Fiction

"**I** know you can do much better than this, Sonia. It seems to me that you're just not trying."

Mr. Peters was holding open my writing journal at the page I had written that day. It had only two short sentences.

"Why don't you write more in your journal?"

"I have nothing to write about."

"I find that hard to believe. Everyone has something to write about."

"Well, *I* don't."

"Why not just write about what's happening in your life?"

"Nothing's happening."

"You could write about your friends."

"I don't *have* any friends."

Mr. Peters gave me a long look. "Then write about *that*. Write about what's inside you—including the things that bother you." He paused. "Here's a special assignment, just for you: think about the one thing that bothers you the most, and write one page about it."

That night, I sat at my bedroom window, looking at the moon. I couldn't do my homework. The blank sheet in my writing journal stared back at me.

I can't write about what bothers me the most. I can't write about Marta and the broken vase, and about how I hate going to school these days. I wish we had never moved here!

But I knew I would explode if I didn't tell someone what was going on.

What if I told what was happening without saying it was about me?

I grabbed a pencil and started to write.

Princess Theodora's kingdom was struck by war and she had to escape to another country. In

the new land, she missed her home. Her whole life changed. Her parents had to work, just like ordinary families do. Theodora's parents wanted to save money so they could return to their own country when the war ended. So they lived very simply. Theodora was lonely. At first she couldn't speak the new language, and she did not understand everything going on around her. She had one friend, Alicia, in her class at school. Alicia's mother looked after Theodora while her parents worked. Once when Theodora was at her friend's house, she dropped a precious antique plate that was worth thousands of dollars. The plate shattered into tiny pieces that could not possibly be put back together. If Alicia's mother found out, Theodora's parents would have to pay for the broken plate. But how? They didn't have enough money. Alicia came up with a solution. She would hide the broken pieces from her mother, but only on one condition: if Theodora would bring her a gift every day. Theodora brought Alicia more and more gifts. But they were never enough. Theodora even had to give up her gold earrings, a gift from her grandmother. But Alicia never seemed pleased. She started making up stories about Theodora and playing tricks on her. Theodora felt scared and even more alone.

I kept writing. It was late when I finished, but I felt strangely calm. Somehow, pouring all my feelings onto paper had given me courage and hope.

I slept without nightmares.

CHAPTER 12

Desperate Measures

"Your homework assignment is excellent, Sonia," Mr. Peters declared. "You have created a strong, serious story. You're a talented writer. I would like you to read your story to the class. And with your permission, I will offer it to our school newspaper."

Normally, I would have been over the moon that Mr. Peters was so pleased with my work. I liked him a lot, and everyone said he was a hard marker.

But reading my story to the class in front of Marta would be a disaster. And having it published in the school paper would be ten times worse. Marta would recognize the story and blame me for making her look bad and getting her into trouble. Everyone would know

how clumsy I am and that my parents are too poor to pay for the damage. My whole family would be shamed.

I didn't know what to say.

"Here are your papers," the teacher announced, walking up and down the aisles to hand them back. "Please take a few minutes to read my comments. Then Sonia will read her story to us."

He smiled broadly as he placed my journal on my desk. It was all I could do to keep from bolting out the door. Instead, I took a deep breath, grabbed the journal and walked out of the classroom. I raced to the lunchroom and went straight to one of the huge garbage cans. Standing over it, I ripped my journal into small pieces and watched them fall in.

Then I returned to class.

"Sonia," called Mr. Peters, "please come up here to read your story."

He turned to the class. "I'd like you all to pay close attention. Sonia has written a brilliant piece that we can learn from."

Brilliant was a word Mr. Peters used only on special occasions. I felt thrilled, embarrassed and miserable all at the same time.

Everyone looked at me expectantly.

"I lost it," I whispered wretchedly.

"Excuse me?" Mr. Peters looked baffled.

"I lost it," I repeated more loudly.

"What do you mean?"

"I can't find it. It vanished."

"It vanished?"

There was a wave of uneasy laughter.

"You *had* it only five minutes ago."

I looked down. In less than a minute, I had gone from being praised and the centre of attention to being the target of laughter. It was my own fault.

"Sonia, this is not funny. You had a wonderful well-written story. How could your journal just vanish? Go look for it. Once you've found it, I want you to read your story to the class."

I sat motionless.

When the lunch bell rang, I ran out before Mr. Peters could stop me.

On my way to the school basement, Marta came up behind me and squeezed my arm. I shrieked.

"So what's this missing story about, huh? I bet it's about me. Give it to me. I want to read what you wrote."

"I don't have it. I threw it in the garbage."

"I don't believe you. Get it out of the garbage and bring it to me!"

"But—I ripped it up. It's probably really soggy and gross by now."

"I don't care. Find it. Or—you know what."

Yeah, I know what.

I returned to the garbage can, fished out all the pieces of my journal and put them in my knapsack.

Mr. Peters' words about my story being good enough to be published in the school newspaper echoed in my mind. I stayed up until very late that night, drying and flattening and taping together the fragments of my story. Now I could read his comments. They smelled of oranges and peanut butter.

Sonia, I am so proud of you. This is beautifully written.

I read through the story again. *Was my writing really that good?* On paper, all my thoughts and feelings were expressed so clearly. Somehow, I had managed to make sense out of what was going on. And now Mr. Peters understood it too.

Maybe I can be a writer when I grow up.

One thing was clear: I was not going to give my story to Marta.

Maybe I will put it in Mr. Peters' mailbox, with a note.

CHAPTER 13

Breaking Point

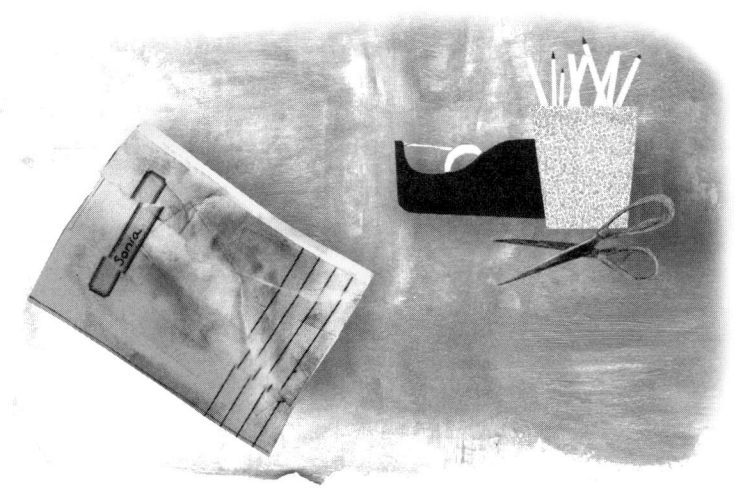

Marta confronted me at breakfast. "So where's the story?"

"I looked for it but I couldn't find it and I'm not looking again," I said, all in one breath. I avoided her eyes. I didn't want to lose my courage. "It probably got dumped out along with the rest of the lunchroom garbage."

"Fine, just give me your breakfast."

"No. I won't."

She took it anyway.

When I got to school, I placed my brilliant, smelly, taped-together story in Mr. Peters' mailbox with a clean, neatly written note.

Dear Mr. Peters,

I was embarrassed to read my story in front of everybody, so I tore it up and threw it in the garbage. Then I changed my mind and glued it back together. Sorry, it looks really bad, and it smells bad too. Thank you for all your nice comments. I can't believe I wrote such a good story. But please don't ask me to read it in class. I don't want it in the school newspaper either. I hope you understand my reasons I think you do.

Sonia

Marta was standing in the hallway, glaring, and wouldn't let me go past. Her arms were folded across her chest, and her face looked like a thundercloud. "Lasagne, you're such a liar! I hate your guts."

Is she spying on me too? I can't take this anymore.

I turned my back on her and ran outside, onto the soccer field. It had just stopped raining, and the ground was wet and muddy. I was cold without my coat, and my feet got soaking wet, but I kept running.

I ran onto the street. A car screeched to a halt, and the driver sounded her horn and yelled, "Hey, watch where you're going!"

A few blocks later, I reached a park. It had started to rain again, but I didn't care. I couldn't return to school. I felt like I was running for my life.

Somehow, I slipped and fell into a huge puddle. I wound up soaked to my waist. I couldn't think what to do next, so I just sat there in the water. *No one cares about me.* I gazed up at the grey sky. *Please let me disappear.*

I don't know how long I sat there.

Suddenly I felt a hand on my shoulder.

"Sonia," uttered Mr. Peters.

I opened my eyes. He was kneeling at the edge of the puddle, wet almost up to his knees.

"What's going on, Sonia? Why did you run away from school? Let's go back to school, find you some dry clothes and get you a cup of hot chocolate. Then you can tell me all about it."

"About what?"

"About why you threw your story in the garbage and then glued it back together. About why you eat your lunches under the stairs or in the furnace room. And about why you ran away from school this morning. It's all the same problem, isn't it?"

I nodded, glad that he cared.

CHAPTER 14

Discovery

"You must tell your parents everything—tonight. I will speak to Marta's grandmother."

I had never seen Mr. Peters so serious.

"But if Mrs. Kaminski finds out about the vase, my parents will have to pay her a lot of money," I protested in alarm.

"Sonia, we will have to let the adults solve that problem themselves. You broke the vase by accident. That kind of accident could happen to anyone. It troubles me that Marta kept you in a trap for so long, and that you didn't tell anyone about it. When someone behaves the way she does, it is called 'bullying.'"

"I know."

"Lots of kids are bullied. And when they are teased or threatened or hurt by another kid or by a group of kids, as you are, they too may be afraid to tell a teacher or a parent. Remember how you felt when I found you in that puddle?"

"Yeah, I felt really alone and kind of desperate."

"Yes, I could see from your story what kind of trouble you were in. Situations like this can end very badly. Do you understand what I mean?"

I wasn't sure. I shook my head.

"Some kids who are bullied feel so much despair that they just want to disappear. They forget about all the people who love them and who could help. Some kids even believe the bully's opinion of them. They think they deserve that kind of treatment. I'm proud of you for recognizing that it was wrong, and for writing about it. What you did takes strength of character."

I wondered if I had the "strength of character" to face all the things that were about to happen. *But wait—once Mrs. Kaminski knows our secret, Marta won't have power over me anymore!*

The most difficult part would be telling my parents about the broken vase.

"Please don't talk to Marta's grandmother before I tell my parents," I begged Mr. Peters.

He gave me a searching look. "Deal. But—" He raised his finger. "Tell your parents *tonight*."

I agreed.

After school, I didn't go to Mrs. Kaminski's place. Instead I went straight home and had the landlady let me into my apartment. I slipped into my bedroom and quickly changed clothes, so my mom wouldn't see the odd outfit Mr. Peters had scavenged from the school's Lost and Found box. I had endured teasing about it all afternoon.

When my mother arrived home, she was surprised to see me. "Why didn't you go to Mrs. Kaminski's after school?"

"Mom, there's something I have to tell you."

"I have something to tell *you* too. Would you like to go shopping with me? We can talk on the way."

I didn't mind going out again, as long as it wasn't to school. It would be fun sharing an umbrella with my mom.

As we walked, Mom explained, "Mrs. Kaminski has to move to Toronto. Marta's mother found a good job there and she asked Mrs. Kaminski and

Marta to join her. They are leaving at the end of this month. Next week will be your last week at their home. We have to find someone else for you to stay with after school."

I didn't know what to think. It seemed like good news. *On the other hand, it would not give my parents very much time to pay back Mrs. Kaminski for the vase.*

"That is why we are going shopping," my mother continued. "I want to buy a present for Mrs. Kaminski. It will be a going-away present, and also to say thank you for looking after you. I see that she likes to collect pretty vases and plates. You can help me pick out something nice." She closed the umbrella as we arrived at the mall. "And now you can tell me what you wanted to say."

"Maybe later, when we've finished shopping."

She nodded. "You are right. It is better to talk at home."

We entered the discount department store and found the Home section. As Mom stood there examining the dishes and vases on display, a saleswoman came up to us.

"If you're looking for a gift, here's something I think you'll like," she declared brightly, leading us to an area near the back of the store. "These vases are very classic and elegant. They sell very well. They look like real antiques, don't they? As a matter of fact, I'm told they are replicas of a valuable centuries-old vase from China."

The vases that she pointed out looked just like Mrs. Kaminski's precious antique vase from China that I had broken. They were the same size and shape and colour as hers, with the same picture of a ship fighting a storm. I reached out to touch one's glossy surface. It was as smooth as I remembered, and had the same fine lines. I turned it over. Glued to the bottom was the same gold label that I had seen on Mrs. Kaminski's vase. It was the same vase exactly!

My legs shook. In an instant, I understood everything. *Mrs. Kaminski's blue vase wasn't shipped to her from China at all—it was bought right here, at the discount store in the mall.* It had not cost a fortune. It was only a cheap imitation, identical to these that had been sitting here the whole time, while Marta threatened me and ate my food. *All that misery and all those nightmares— for nothing!*

I struggled to hide my anger. I reminded myself to breathe, and then counted to ten in my head.

I turned to my mother. "Please, Mom, I really think we should give this vase to Mrs. Kaminski. It's the perfect gift. I *know* she'd like it. It's exactly her taste."

The saleswoman smiled and turned to my mom. "Your daughter seems to have made up her mind."

"Sonia is very artistic. She has made a good decision. I will buy this vase." My mom gave my hand an affectionate squeeze.

I insisted upon carrying the bag home myself. I held it carefully.

"What did you want to talk about, dear?" Mom asked when we returned home.

"Nothing," I replied. "It's okay."

CHAPTER 15

Moving On

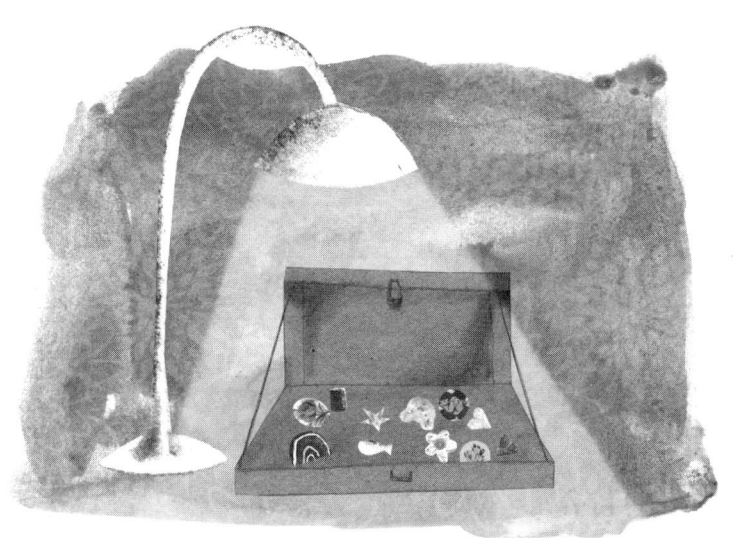

At Mrs. Kaminski's the next day, there was no mention of moving. There were no suitcases or boxes around anywhere; there was no sign of anything out of the ordinary.

Mrs. Kaminski served our breakfast and returned to her cabbage rolls and TV.

I pretended that nothing had changed. I didn't touch my breakfast plate; I was waiting for Marta to reach for it after she finished hers. Looking forward to that moment filled me with such nervous excitement that my hands were shaking. I hid them under the table.

Marta wiped the last of the sour cream from her plate with the last forkful of omelette, then glared at me. "Well? Haven't you learned by now to slide your plate over to me as soon as I'm finished with mine? I can't believe I still have to tell you!"

My big moment had come, but I didn't want to spend it just like that. I wanted it to be perfect.

"Have you gone deaf? What's your problem, Lasagne?"

"I am not giving you my breakfast today." Before she could grab it, I cut a large piece of my omelette, dipped it generously into the sour cream, and chewed slowly. Then I tore a big piece off the fresh-baked bun and chewed that even more slowly. I closed my eyes so I could enjoy my breakfast without having to see Marta.

When I opened my eyes, her face was full of disbelief.

"*You can't do that!* You can't eat your whole breakfast, just like that! You're supposed to give it to me!"

I did not reply.

"Well then, you're gonna be sorry." Her tone was a little less confident than before. "I'll just go straight into the kitchen and tell my grandma that you broke her precious vase."

I stood up. "As a matter of fact, I was about to tell her myself."

I strode to the kitchen and called, "Mrs. Kaminski, may I talk to you for a minute?"

Mrs. Kaminski wiped her hands on her apron and looked up.

"Yes? What is it?"

I stole a glance at Marta, who was trailing me. She looked pale.

"I have to tell you something I've been hiding for a long time. I was afraid you would be angry."

Mrs. Kaminski waited for me to find my voice. The TV blared behind her.

"I broke your beautiful blue vase. It was an accident. I'm really sorry. I should have told you sooner."

"Which vase was it?" she asked, suddenly concerned.

"The blue vase that was shipped to you all the way from China.The expensive one with the picture of a ship in a storm."

Mrs. Kaminski laughed in relief. "Oh, that one! Don't worry—I already knew about it. Marta told me, the same day it happened."

I shot a look at Marta.

"Where did you get the idea that the vase was valuable? I only paid a few dollars for it," Mrs. Kaminski continued. "I asked Marta to tell you not to be concerned about breaking it."

Marta looked scared and helpless now. She waited to see what would happen next.

She's trapped—and I'm free!

To my surprise, the victory didn't give me much satisfaction. Even though Marta deserved to be taught a lesson, I chose not to say anything. I didn't need to. My problem had been solved.

"Girls, time to go to school." Mrs. Kaminski turned toward the kitchen, and Marta and I left.

We walked all the way to school without a word.

I told Mr. Peters the end of my story.

"I'm pleased that the situation has been dealt with. As you see, you have more courage than you realized. But I still have a duty to report Marta's behaviour to her grandmother, to prevent Marta from hurting others."

In a way, I feel sorry for Marta. What would make her want to treat me that way?

I just want to have friends and to be a good writer.

During the three weeks before she moved to Toronto, Marta stopped being mean to me at school. Maybe she was ashamed of her actions, now that her grandmother and the teachers knew about them. Even if she had started bothering me again, I would have just walked away.

Marta's friends also stopped picking on me.

My mother gave Mrs. Kaminski her good-bye present and told her that I had chosen it.

On her last day at school, Marta returned my eraser collection. Even though it had been mine to begin with, I felt that I had won it.

KATARINA JOVANOVIC is a recipient of the Christie Harris Children's Literature Prize for *The King Has Goat Ears*. She teaches education in Vancouver. She lives in Vancouver with her husband and two daughters.

JOSÉE BISAILLON has won many awards for her illustration work and she was a finalist for the Governor General's Literary Award in 2008 and 2010. She lives in Montreal with her husband and three charming children. She loves drawing cats and cutting things out of any scrap of paper she can get her hands on.

. . .